101 INCREDIBLE
AND FUN FACTS ABOUT
JAPAN

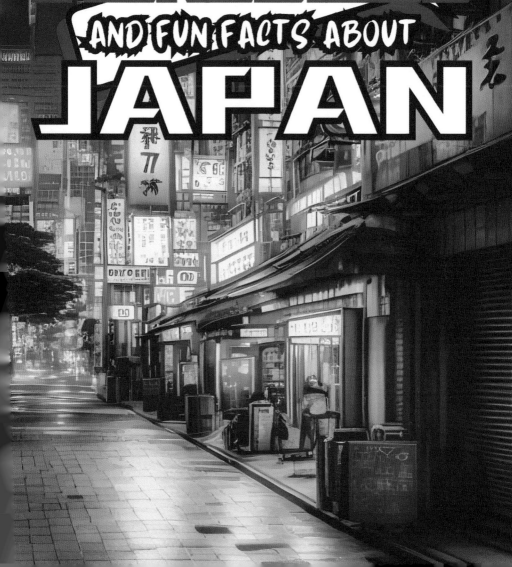

THANK YOU FOR PURCHASING THIS NOTEBOOK OF 101 SUPER COOL FACTS ABOUT JAPAN!

As a small independent publisher, every one of your comments shapes our future publications. We look forward to reading your feedback!

ありがとう

Copyright © 2024 Funmama Editing

Welcome to the Super Know-It-All Challenge!

Ready to dive into a world of amazing and fun facts?
This book is packed with **101 awesome facts** about Japan and here's a special challenge
just for you!
How many of these facts do you already know?
Track your score, compare with friends, and see how much you really know!

0 to 10 facts: Explorer Level

Not a ton, but don't worry, 70 % of people start right here!
Ask your friends, you'll see you're not alone.
Plus, you'll only get smarter as you keep reading!

11 to 30 facts: Adventurer Level

You're on the right track! You already know some cool stuff and
are doing great. Keep going, and soon you could be a real fact champion!

31 to 60 facts: Expert Level

Wow, now you're really standing out! You know a lot, and you're well on
your way to becoming a champion. Just a little more for the next level!

61 to 90 facts: Champion Level

Impressive! You're one of the best, and your knowledge will surprise others.
Just a few more facts to reach the ultimate level!

91 to 101 facts: Legend Level

Amazing! Congratulations! You're a true legend!
Only 0,01% of people know as much as you do! Share your knowledge and
inspire your friends!

Japan has amazing gadgets! There are millions of vending machines that sell everything from live lobsters to underwear. Their high-tech toilets have tons of features, and they even have 'silent' karaoke microphones. To save space, they use multi-level parking lots.

They have fascinating traditions and cultural quirks! For example, 'inemuri' means taking a short nap at work, which is seen as a sign of dedication. They politely slurp their noodles to show they're enjoying the meal, and they avoid the number 4 because it's considered bad luck.

Japan, nicknamed the 'Land of the Rising Sun,' is a magical archipelago made up of over 6,800 islands! The largest ones, like Honshu, Hokkaido, Kyushu, and Shikoku, make up 97% of its land.

There are 47 prefectures, with over 70% being mountainous. Imagine a landscape where mountains rise proudly, with the majestic Mount Fuji, the highest peak, reaching 3,776 meters! But watch out, the ground might sometimes shake a bit, with over 1,500 earthquakes every year.

Power is shared between a prime minister, who runs the government, and an emperor. But the emperor doesn't have the same power as in manga! He's more of a symbol, like a movie star, but for the country.

Each season brings its own magic and surprises! Whether it's spring with its cherry blossoms, the hot and humid summer, the colorful autumn, or the snowy winter, there's always something special to discover. And with each season comes a new range of flavors, from fresh spring treats to comforting winter dishes.

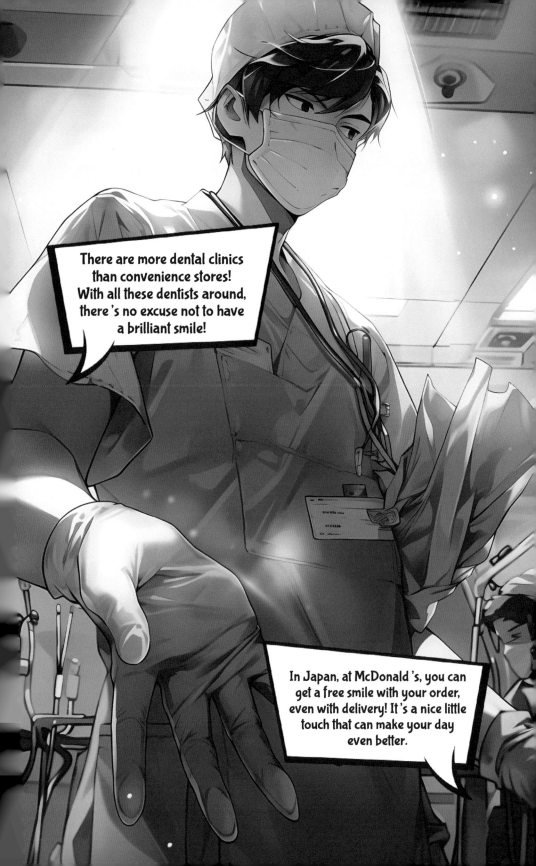

A package delivery company in Japan has found a cute and practical way to help visually impaired people.
Their delivery notices have cat logos and borders shaped like cat ears to make them easier to identify. It's both useful and super cute!

If you miss a delivery, the delivery person leaves a number to call for rescheduling within a 2-hour window! If you call before 6-8 PM (depending on the company), they can often redeliver the same day.
Sometimes, the number even directly reaches the delivery person in their truck.
Super convenient!

Did you know that bamboo is one of the fastest-growing plants in the world? In Japan, some species of bamboo can grow up to a meter a day! This plant grows almost as fast as you do during a growth spurt!

Young bamboo shoots are incredibly strong! They can break through wood, stone, and sometimes even concrete! They're like plant superheroes, capable of smashing through walls to reach the light!

There are only two species of wild cats in Japan, and you'll only find them on remote islands. They're like island adventurers, living far from everyone else in their own little secret paradises!

Ah, the Maneki Neko! A true star in the world of cats in Japan for centuries! You can easily recognize it by its raised paw that waves to greet you. It's also known as the 'Fortune Cat' or 'Lucky Cat,' and it's full of symbols of good luck. If you see a calico Maneki Neko (with a tricolored coat), it's a sign of good fortune. Whether its paw is raised on the left or right, it's always a positive sign for more wealth and luck

Tokyo is the most populous city in the world, home to about 10% of Japan's population. When you include the Greater Tokyo Metropolitan Area, it totals 38 million people, which is 30% of Japan's entire population!

Japan has one of the lowest crime rates in the world, making it one of the safest countries. The most common crimes are minor, like bike or umbrella theft. People feel so safe that they often leave their belongings unattended.

Japan, including its capital Tokyo, is famous for its ultra-clean and litter-free streets. The Japanese are incredibly committed to cleanliness, and it shows everywhere! Every street corner is always spotless, like a movie scene where everything shines!

To master Japanese, it takes about 2,200 hours of study! In everyday life, Japanese people use four different writing systems. It's a real challenge, but it makes the language super interesting!

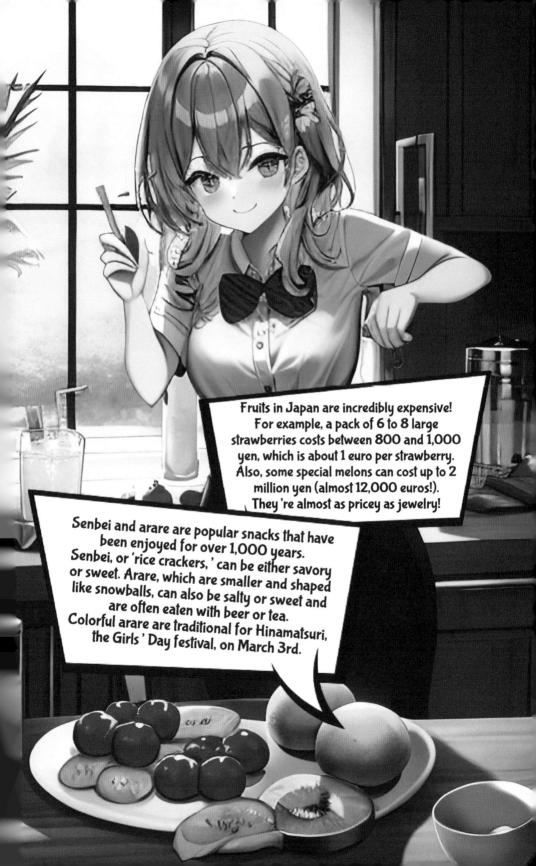

Fruits in Japan are incredibly expensive!
For example, a pack of 6 to 8 large
strawberries costs between 800 and 1,000
yen, which is about 1 euro per strawberry.
Also, some special melons can cost up to 2
million yen (almost 12,000 euros!).
They're almost as pricey as jewelry!

Senbei and arare are popular snacks that have
been enjoyed for over 1,000 years.
Senbei, or 'rice crackers,' can be either savory
or sweet. Arare, which are smaller and shaped
like snowballs, can also be salty or sweet and
are often eaten with beer or tea.
Colorful arare are traditional for Hinamatsuri,
the Girls' Day festival, on March 3rd.

Episode 38 of the first season of Pokémon sent nearly 700 kids to the hospital. They experienced dizziness, vomiting, and even seizures.
The cause? A Pikachu battle in cyberspace with very intense red and blue flashes.

Do you know 'Kinnikuman'? It's a cult manga in Japan that tells the story of Prince Suguru. Sent as a baby into a space garbage chute, he grows up to become a Japanese superhero. It's a wild adventure full of superpowers that has captivated millions of fans!

Japanese people live very long lives thanks to their healthy diet. The problem is, while everyone is living longer, the population isn't renewing itself as much. But hey, we can't fault them for living a long time, right? Over 50,000 Japanese have reached the age of 100 on the Japanese archipelago. In France, there are just over 20,000.

There's a village called Nagoro, located on Tokushima Island, that is gradually emptying of its inhabitants. But one devoted resident, Tsukimi Ayano, decided not to let her village become a ghost town! She came up with a surprising idea: replacing each person who leaves with a doll. It's both cute and a little eerie, don't you think?

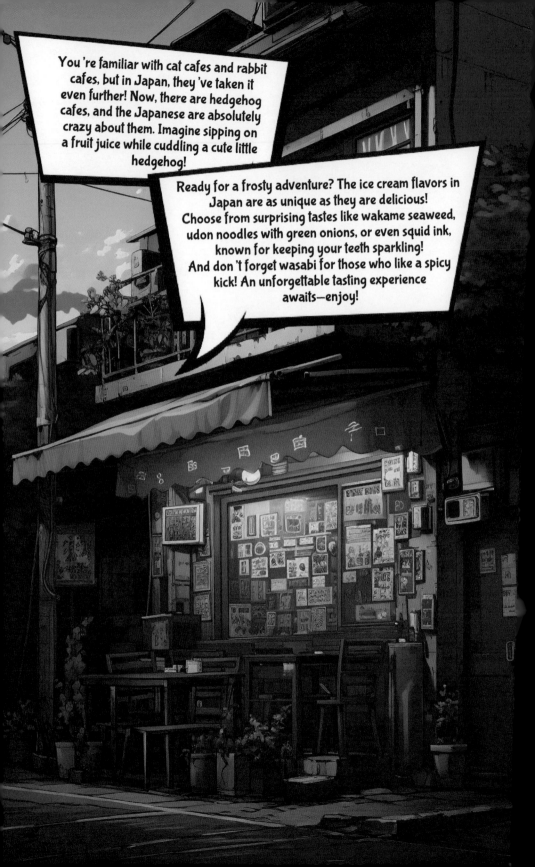

You're familiar with cat cafes and rabbit cafes, but in Japan, they've taken it even further! Now, there are hedgehog cafes, and the Japanese are absolutely crazy about them. Imagine sipping on a fruit juice while cuddling a cute little hedgehog!

Ready for a frosty adventure? The ice cream flavors in Japan are as unique as they are delicious! Choose from surprising tastes like wakame seaweed, udon noodles with green onions, or even squid ink, known for keeping your teeth sparkling! And don't forget wasabi for those who like a spicy kick! An unforgettable tasting experience awaits—enjoy!

In Japan, public trash cans are quite rare, and there's a reason for that! In 1995, a cult caused chaos in Tokyo's subway with sarin gas. Since then, trash cans have been removed to prevent hiding spots for wrongdoers. But don't worry, the Japanese are experts at keeping public spaces clean. Plus, who needs a trash can when you have pockets?

Some trash cans are equipped with a reward system to encourage recycling.
When you dispose of a bottle or can in the correct compartment, the trash can gives you a discount voucher or a ticket that can be exchanged for a gift. It's a fun way to motivate everyone to participate in recycling!

There are 'trash hunters,' modern heroes who patrol the streets, parks, and public places to hunt down every piece of litter.
Their mission?
To maintain spotless cleanliness!

Japanese supporters made a huge impression on cleanliness during the 2018 World Cup! After the matches, they stayed behind to help clean the stands!

During the 2022 World Cup, Japan's surprise victory over Spain sparked huge, joyful gatherings in Tokyo. Supporters dressed as samurais danced and sang in the streets starting at 6 a.m.

In the city of Shimabara, on Kyushu Island, the drainage canal water is so clean that koi carp live in it. After a tsunami in 1792, fresh water springs emerged, flowing through the city. Today, these waters are so pure that fish swim freely in them!

In Japan, there are over 300 multi-directional crosswalks where you can cross in all directions.
The most famous one is in the Shibuya district of Tokyo. Nearly 3,000 pedestrians cross simultaneously during the two-minute green light!

Printed in Great Britain
by Amazon

54837995R00032